Harvesting Love

Jax Wilder

Harvesting Love © 2024 by Jax Wilder
Rainbow Quartz Publishing

RAINBOW QUARTZ PUBLISHING

COVER ART BY RAINBOW QUARTZ PUBLISHING
IG: RAINBOW QUARTZ PUBLISHING

HTTPS://RQPUBLISHING.COM/

ISBN: 978-1-961714-10-6

For the gays and the theys who struggle with the holidays, this book is for you. You are seen and you are loved.

1
Lea

A loud clamor, followed by what sounded like a million books tumbling over, echoed from the back of the store. I dropped my cell phone on the desk and sprinted toward the sound.

I rounded the back wall corner and saw Park on the ground, covered in books. Looking up, I saw the top two shelves had completely toppled.

"Are you okay?" I asked as I bent over and attempted to unbury poor Park. He better be okay. He's my one and only employee.

"I think so," Park said, rubbing his head.

"What happened?"

"I was trying to get the overstock copies of *From the 911 Files* by Jackson Anhalt from the top shelf, since it's been selling so well lately, and move them to the front feature section. I thought I could grab it without using the stool, and here we are." Park got up and rubbed his head.

"Do I have to go over company policy on safety again? Show you the cheesy 80s videotapes on trips, slips, and falls? We always use the stool, Park," I used my snarkiest tone of voice, so he knew I was not seriously mad, but come on, kid. You've been here for how long? These shelves are old and sturdy, but they have their limits.

"I guess I'll have to review the tapes again. This bump on my head will have to serve as the instant reminder," Park laughed a little.

"Do you need to go to urgent care or anything?" I asked.

"No, no, I'm fine," Park's stoicism always leaves me uncertain if he is hurt.

"I'll fill out an incident form later for this anyway, just to be sure. I'm going to head back to the front real quick. I dropped my phone in my haste," I said and turned around.

"I'll grab the stool and clean this up, don't worry," Park said.

"Oh, it's fine. I'll be right back," I assured him.

"I got it. You stay up front to help customers. It was my dumb mistake, and I can clean it up. It'll give me an opportunity to dust those upper shelves. It'll be another reminder to always use the stool," Park smiled, and it was reassuring enough for me to give in.

"Okay, but if you want some help, I don't mind at all," I offered in a last-ditch effort.

As the owner of a small business, having my sole employee get injured on the job could break me. Sure,

I have my husband, Alex, who could help, but he gets extremely busy at work around the holidays.

In the seaside town of Coral Cove, there aren't many people actively seeking part-time work at a small, independent bookstore. At Spellbound Stories, we cater primarily to the independently wealthy, the elderly/retired folks, and tourists looking to escape it all.

Back at the desk, I grabbed my phone and inspected it for any damage. Thankfully, it was all in one piece. I flipped through my screens, but I didn't remember what I was doing before the crash. I locked my screen and set it down.

"Is your colleague okay?" an elderly woman appeared seemingly out of nowhere, right in front of me.

Having not seen her before today, I stifled a scream and replied, "Huuuhh... uhhhh, yeah. Yes. Park is fine."

"I didn't mean to frighten you, dear," she smiled.

She had the sweetest eyes I had ever seen. They were a deep brown, filled with wisdom and compassion. She had a sparkle and a magical quality about her that was difficult to describe. She drew me in like a magnet with her captivating presence. I somehow knew she gave the warmest, most comforting hugs.

"I just didn't see you walk up," I smiled back. "I'm sorry. Have we met before?"

"I don't think so. This is my first time in the shop. Actually, this is my first time to Coral Cove," she said.

"Well, welcome to town. I hope that you're enjoying yourself. We're not a large town, but what we lack in size, we more than make up for in heart and charm," I said proudly.

"It has been absolutely magical, and I've only just arrived this morning," she said. "I guess that's what drew me here."

The old lady gently dropped a few books, all by famed author Miranda Levi, onto the desk. *Mo(ther) Na(ture), From a Youth A Fountain Did Flow*, and its sequel *The Sea Withdrew*.

"Great choices. This one just came out," I said as I held up the sequel in the Fountain series. "I started it but haven't finished it yet."

"I have heard great things about this author, and when I saw them in your featured section, I knew I had to grab them all," the old lady said.

As I rang her up, she kept turning towards the back of the store, towards Park, and although we didn't have a visual on him, somehow it felt like she was staring at him. She turned back as I read her total aloud, and then she handed me some crisp new bills. I made her change and felt terrible about giving her the crusty bills sitting in the register for who knows how long. She was still staring towards the back of the store.

"Here's your change," I said to catch her attention.

She turned back towards me and gave me a friendly stare. "You should check on him again."

"I will," I promised.

"He may be okay physically, but I sense there's more going on. The holidays can be a hard time for folks. He might need someone to check in on his soul."

It was as if she had known us our entire lives. The old woman and I stood for a few moments in comfortable silence, staring intensely into each other's eyes. Such an experience would freak me out with anyone else, but somehow it felt as natural as breathing with her. I shook my head slightly and handed her a bag.

Remembering we have a flyer for Miranda Levi's new releases, I turned around to grab the shelf behind me. I flipped through a few author announcements before finding the right one. It only took about three seconds.

I turned around to hand the older woman the flyer, but she was gone.

Disappeared.

The bell above the door didn't even ring. Just as fast as she appeared in my peripheral, she had vanished.

2
Park

Thankfully, Lea was working today. I'm already embarrassed beyond belief about my accident, but having a customer find me instead would be absolutely mortifying. Lea will probably never bring this up again. She is a wonderful person and an even greater boss.

With my background and education, I could have easily chosen to stay working for a large publishing company like I did before moving to Coral Cove. I had just finished one of the most brutal fiscal years at work and was desperate for a break. I came to Coral Cove on the first vacation I'd been on in years.

I fell deeply in love with the magic and energy surrounding this place. It was almost like a vortex pulling at my soul, telling me I needed to make this place my home.

I knew I would find a home here.

I knew I would find community here.

I went home, submitted my two weeks to my boss, packed up what I could fit in my car, sold everything else, and moved to Coral Cove.

I knew the town would take care of me.

I knew I would find the job of my dreams.

I knew I needed the stool to reach the top shelf. This thought made me giggle to myself. I have just been so distracted this week.

I looked myself over for any signs of bruising from the fall. Feeling none, I walked into the stockroom, where we kept our measly number of tools. I grabbed a hammer, a couple of small nails, a little vial of superglue, and cleaning wipes.

Walking back to the pile of books, I realized I had forgotten the most important tool I would need—the stool. I threw my head back and groaned slightly. I slapped my hand across my face, balanced the tools on another shelf, and returned to grab the stool.

I repaired the shelves. Lucky for me, it went by quickly. They had not broken, just become loose.

With a few taps of the hammer and a new nail on the top shelf's bracket support, it was as good as new.

My mind wandered as I wiped the layers of dust off the top of the shelving unit. Thanksgiving was right around the corner, and I dreaded heading back home. I love my family with all my heart. My sisters are my life, but sometimes being around them hurts.

Out of the corner of my eye, I saw Lea approaching. I shook away my thoughts and continued purposefully wiping. Lea zig-zagged through the aisles, which caught my full attention.

As she approached, I stopped wiping and climbed down off the stool.

"Are you good?" I asked.

"Did you see an older lady come back here?" Lea asked, looking around at the back angles, which would expose both sides of the store.

"No," I said. "I haven't seen anyone back here at all."

"I just made a sale, and I turned around to hand her this flyer, and she was gone."

"Oh. Maybe she didn't want your sales pitch and booked it." I gently elbowed her.

"Ha. Ha. But for real, the bell above the door didn't ring. I thought for sure she still had to be in here." Lea scanned the store.

"Weird. Maybe we've just gotten so used to tuning it out? I feel like I never hear it anymore," I offered some plausibility.

"I suppose," Lea said, unsure. Despite that, it really weirded me out. I even checked the computer for her sale to ensure I didn't imagine the whole thing.

I laughed a little at this. "No phantom money?"

"Nope. Real crisp, legal tender," Lea said with a smile.

"I don't know what to tell you," I said. "I was in the back getting tools and the stool, so I could have missed someone while back there."

"Eh, it's all good. Just weird." She paused momentarily, then added, "Are you okay?"

"Huh?" I had forgotten about the fall already. "Oh, yeah. I checked myself over. All good."

I showed her my arms and hands and did a twirl for her.

"I'm glad, but are you okay in general?" Lea left the question hanging.

"What do you mean?" I asked.

"I dunno. You seemed a little distracted today, and I wondered if you had a lot on your mind or something. You can always talk to me, you know." Lea smiled. "I'm not like a regular boss. I'm a cool boss." She shrugged a shoulder in a remarkable Amy Poehler impression.

"Ha. I know," I thought about it. Maybe it would be nice to talk to Lea. "I have been thinking a lot about Thanksgiving. Heading back to my mom's place has been giving me a lot of anxiety."

"Oh?"

"Yeah. I love my family, but the holidays can be stressful with everyone around," I debated giving her more of the story, but decided against it.

"I can certainly understand that. Remember to give yourself grace and space."

"Nice rhyme," I cut her off.

"I know, right?" She ran her fingers through her long red hair. "Seriously though, allow yourself to feel how you're going to feel so you can process those emotions. Excuse yourself if it all becomes too much and go for a walk. Get some fresh air and walk around the block or something."

"Grace and space," I repeated. "I like that." I turned around and looked at the mass of books at my feet that still needed sorting, and returned to the shelves. My shoulder received a gentle pat.

"And if you need anything else or you just want someone to talk to, you can always give me a call," Lea said from behind me. "I'm not just the boss; you're my friend, and I care about you."

"Thank you, Lea," I turned and faced her. "Thank you. It'll be alright. I will be alright. I should get back to sorting these." I thumbed behind me.

"Offer still stands if you want me to help you clean up things." Lea lingered for an answer.

"Ha. No. You keep searching for your old lady ghost," I smiled.

"It happened! I promise," Lea huffed and left me to my pile.

3
Ben

"Where are you going on your vacation?" Rachel asked.

"A little town called Coral Cove," I said, opening the confirmation email for the hotel to double-check the dates. Even though I checked the dates three times after I booked it. "My anxiousness wants everything to be perfect. I keep checking that I booked the right flights, checking the hotel dates, and making sure I booked the rental car at the right airport."

"Awww. It's going to be great. Did you book the wrong stuff on the last trip?" Rachel asked.

"No. I have never made a huge mistake like that," I say, a bit indignant. "I just want everything to be perfect."

"That's a lot of pressure for a Thanksgiving adventure. I'm assuming Jeremy is going with you?" Rachel asked.

"Yes," I said with a smile.

Rachel is my best friend at work and knows almost everything about me. Usually, I keep my guard up at work with co-workers. Maintaining a work/life balance is essential for me. Earlier in my career, I jumped from line-level to management at a different company, and it was a living hell. People who I thought were my friends suddenly couldn't wait to sink their teeth into my neck. Anything I said or did as their equal was now used against me at every turn as their boss.

"How was your weekend, Ben?"

"Fine. Thank you."

"Did you do anything fun?"

"Nope. Just sat around excited to be back here again on Monday."

"Mondays, amirite?"

"Hump day."

Clichés upon clichés are all anyone will ever get out of me. No one knows what they can't immediately see. They could tell I was a minority. They didn't know I was gay. They could see my ringless fingers and assume I wasn't married, but I wouldn't tell them about my boyfriend.

Then, I met Rachel.

She tore down my walls slowly at first. Rachel and I are from the same hood and know all the same people. We were in the trenches together. I knew where she came from and how we grew up. She understood my past, too. I knew she was someone I could trust.

"I haven't heard of Coral Cove before. Where is it?" Rachel asked.

"It's on the coast. Honestly, it's some white bread, picturesque, let's go look at some bridges n' shit kind of town," I laughed, and Rachel joined in.

"What made you pick that place?" Rachel asked through her laughter.

"It has been a place that Jeremy has romanticized for years. He's been talking about it for as long as we've been together, and we just haven't been able to make it work with our schedules."

"Oh, I get it. You're going for him. That's very romantic of you, Ben. I'm impressed."

"That's not everything," I smiled.

"Oh?" Rachel moved to the edge of her seat.

"I'm going to ask him to marry me."

Rachel's eyes widened, and she let out an excited squeal. "Ben! That's amazing! Do you have everything planned out? How are you going to do it?"

"I have a few ideas," I said, my smile widening. "I'm thinking of doing it on one of the scenic bridges at sunset. Jeremy loves sunsets, and I think it will be perfect."

"That sounds beautiful," Rachel said, her eyes sparkling with excitement. "He's going to love it. You both deserve all the happiness in the world."

"Thanks, Rachel. That means a lot," I said, feeling a warmth spread through me.

"I'm so happy for you," Rachel said, giving me a quick hug. "You better text me as soon as you do it. I want to know everything!"

"I will," I promised, feeling a mix of nerves and excitement. "Now, I just have to make sure everything goes according to plan."

Rachel smiled. "It will. And even if it doesn't, it will still be perfect because it's about the two of you."

I nodded, taking a deep breath. "You're right. It's going to be amazing."

As Rachel walked back to her desk, I glanced at the confirmation email once more, double-checking the details. Coral Cove was going to be the perfect place to start this new chapter in our lives. I could picture the look on Jeremy's face when I asked him to marry me, and I couldn't wait to make that moment a reality.

4
Park

A wave of relief washed over me as I placed the last book on the shelf. I gave the shelf a good tug to ensure that it was still stable. It didn't move.

"Phew," I said, stretching.

I looked down at my watch. It took me over an hour to clean up that mess. I grabbed the stack of *From the 911 Files* I left in a neat pile on the floor and walked toward the front of the store where we keep our Featured Books section. While stacking the books neatly, I mentally noted which books needed restocking. Suddenly, I caught movement out of the corner of my eye.

"Weren't you supposed to leave like 15 minutes ago?" I asked Lea.

"Yeah, but it's okay. I forgot to submit the order this morning, so it was good I was still here," Lea said.

"I was listening for the bell. You didn't have to stick around on my behalf," I said.

"Again, it's all good. I'm just heading out now. Alex isn't even home for another hour or so, anyway. I filled out that incident form for you. Read it over, add anything you'd like, and leave it on my desk upstairs. I just need to have it for the insurance company in case you hurt tomorrow," Lea said matter-of-factly.

"I said I'm fine." I didn't mean to sound as annoyed as it came out.

"I understand, but I care about you and expect you to take care of yourself if you feel sore tomorrow," Lea grabbed my arm and looked into my eyes. "You will go see a doctor. Right?"

"Yes," I said, placating her.

"Alright, have a good night. I'm out of here." Lea grabbed her bag from the upstairs office and waved goodbye to me as she shuffled out of the store.

I noted the bell dinged as she left. Once when she pulled the door open and again when it swung closed.

Wednesday nights were my usual closing nights. Tonight would be unique because we would close for the entire weekend, so I'd be sure to power down everything.

Tomorrow was Thanksgiving. Everything in Coral Cove would be closed. Lea and I have been vehemently against working on Black Friday. It's an absolute garbage holiday plagued by consumerism and greed. Traditionally, Coral Cove didn't have a lot of shoppers on Black Friday. Shoppers turned mainly to the big box names in the cities.

Lea decided long ago that we'd be closed on Black Friday. She never was one for the holidays, but recently, she's changed her tone. She values family time more, so we close for the entire weekend.

I think that's her husband, Alex, rubbing off on her.

After finishing my shift, I would go home, pack my bags, and get a good night's sleep before starting the five-hour drive to my mother's house.

I grabbed a few more books and moved them from the desk to the feature shelf. I rearranged a few by color to make it more pleasing to the eye.

The bell jingled.

"Welcome! Let me know if you need any help to find anything," I told the couple as they entered the shop.

"Thank you," the guy said as they started browsing.

The bell jingled.

I looked over as a tall, handsome man entered the store. He was one of the sexiest humans I have ever seen. Dark caramel skin, beautiful brown eyes, tight clothes rippling over shoulder muscles, bulging pecs, and the waist of a gymnast.

I stumbled over my words. "Welcome in. The store. Hi. Help if you need." I collected myself and cleared my throat. "Welcome! Let me know if you need help finding anything."

I turned to hide behind the counter. My cheeks were hot and, I'm sure, bright red.

"Actually, I need some help. Do you guys have gift cards?" he asked.

"We do! I can do that for that." My gods, what was wrong with me? *I can do that for you.* I'm such a dumbass.

He chuckled a little, cocked his head, and walked up to the register.

"These are the gift card options," I pointed to the various cards on the rack. Lea had bought a bunch of holiday-themed cards. Some for Valentine's Day, Thanksgiving, birthdays, and a ton of Christmas ones.

"I think I'll take this one," the sexy man grabbed one of the more generic *A Gift For You* cards. A carryover from before Lea caught the holiday bug.

"Very good. How much would you like to put on it?" I asked and reached out to grab the card from him. His fingers brushed against mine. It was as if a lightning bolt ran up my spine.

I shook it off and looked into his eyes again.

He scrunched up his nose and kind of looked around. "I'm not sure. I'm going to be honest. I'm not much of a reader. How much are books these days?"

"Umm, it really varies. What kind of books does— uh—the recipient like?" I can't formulate words or thoughts to save my life around this hunk of a man.

"Oh, it's for my wife," he said.

A twinge of pain, like a thousand knives, went through my chest.

"She likes girly books and romance garbage," he said.

It took a lot of my restraint not to comment on the words "romance garbage," but I composed myself before saying, "Okay, that gives me a good idea. Generally, those novels are quite popular and range between the ten and thirty-dollar range depending on the author, if it's hardback or paperback, or a mass-produced paperback. Usually, costs more for the audiobooks on CD. But we've got it all."

"I'll do $100 then. That way, she can get a few of them. She loves this store," he said, handing me his credit card.

"Alright, sounds good." I finished processing the transaction and loading up the gift card. I handed him back his credit card. "Here's an envelope that the gift cards fit into. Do you need a bag as well?"

"Naw, that's good as it is," he smiled, and I went weak at the knees again. Such a dazzling smile. That woman is a lucky bitch. Even if she married an idiot who doesn't read.

The handsome stranger walked out of the store, and I watched the cheeks on his behind as he darted across the road. I didn't notice but was fanning my face with my hand.

I looked over down the central aisle of the store and realized that the female half of the couple that came in caught me staring at the giant hunk of a man.

Mortified, I shook my head and tried to turn and hide anywhere.

She laughed and moved towards me.

"Don't be embarrassed, baby. I was getting so wet over that fine ass man that we're gonna need a mop in aisle two over there."

I blushed even more, unsure how to respond. "Glad I'm not the only one," I finally said, attempting a laugh. "Can I help you find anything?"

5
Ben

After work, I hurried home and started packing for the weekend adventure. I pulled an old, dirty box from the back of my closet. I reached for the brown paper bag buried at the bottom of the nonsense pile of junk I should eventually sort through and prune from the box.

Inside the paper bag was a velvet ring box. I opened the latch, cracked open the lid, and stared down at the simple yet elegant diamond-encrusted band I was going to ask the love of my life to accept. I shut the lid and carefully wrapped it in a sock, so it wasn't obvious that I was hiding anything. I placed the sock in my suitcase near the top. I didn't want him to find it before I was ready.

After packing our clothes, I rechecked the flights to ensure they were on time. We were good to go. I cleaned up the kitchen, emptied the dishwasher, and took out the trash before Jeremy arrived. Additionally, I arranged for his favorite pizza to be delivered from Uber Eats. I just cleaned this kitchen; I wouldn't mess it up again by cooking.

After returning to the apartment and taking the garbage to the dumpster, I checked my phone for the delivery estimate. Less than a minute away. Perfect.

"Wait, it was going to take a half-hour to get here," I said, looking again at my phone. Jeremy should have been home 15 minutes ago.

I shrugged it off. He probably got held over for a few minutes. It's the day before vacation. He probably had to wrap some things up before the long weekend.

The pizza arrived, and I threw it in the oven to keep it warm. I picked up the bathroom while waiting for Jeremy to get home. I had a constructive habit of cleaning up my house before a vacation. It feels good to come home to a clean house.

I finished scrubbing the toilet and washing my hands in the hottest water I could stand. I dried them off and headed back into the living room. I searched around. Still no Jeremy.

I grabbed my phone and looked at the time.

"He's never been an hour late without texting or calling me," I said. I sent him a quick text message.

> **Me:** Hey babe, where are you? I got us some pizza. It's in the oven warming up for us.

I turned on the TV and waited for his reply. Nothing. I texted Rachel.

Me: Jeremy is over an hour late getting home from work. I haven't heard from him. I'm starting to get worried.

My phone blooped.

> **Rachel:** He probably got held up at work. The day before vacation. Did you try calling him?

Rachel's text confirmed my thoughts.

> **Me:** Not yet. I'm gonna give him another half hour or so. I don't like to bother him when he's working.

> **Rachel:** That's a good plan.

I barely watched the episode. I kept staring at my phone, waiting for a text or a call. When the episode ended, a sinking, horrible feeling overwhelmed me. My hands shook as I clicked on Jeremy's number to dial.

The phone rang. And rang. And rang. Voicemail. Fuck.

I started pacing. I didn't know what else to do. Jeremy shared my sentiments about work/life balance. None of our close friends worked with him. They would be of no use. I knew his boss's name was Matt, but I didn't have his number.

I couldn't do much of anything. I texted Rachel a few more times. She did her best to comfort me, but I could tell she was also getting concerned.

Another hour went by. I sent at least forty panic texts to Jeremy, begging and pleading with him to text or call me back. There was a knock at the door.

My whole body shook as I walked to the door. I opened it slowly and saw a deputy drenched from the rain.

"Are you Ben Dawson?" he asked.

"Yes," I trembled.

"I am sorry to tell you this, but there has been an accident."

The words hung in the air, thick and suffocating. My heart pounded in my chest as I struggled to process what the deputy had just said. An accident. My mind raced with possibilities, each more horrifying than the last.

"Jeremy?" I whispered, my voice barely audible.

The deputy nodded solemnly. "Yes, sir."

6
Park

After such a long drive, I was not prepared for the energy of my mother's house. Nieces, nephews, sisters, aunties, and uncles bombarded me as soon as I walked in the door. Forty or so hugs later, I finally made it to my mother, who was working away in the kitchen. She looked up from peeling her green beans, and her eyes lit up.

"Park, my baby!" Her arms outstretched, Mom started towards me.

I grabbed my mother and held her deeply in a squeeze. "How are you, my son?"

"Exhausted. Do you have any cold brew?" I asked.

"Yes, in the fridge." Mom pointed to the refrigerator and returned to her beans.

I knew better than to ask if she needed any help in the kitchen. We all knew better. The best way to help my mom in the kitchen was to stay out of her kitchen. I grabbed a can of cold brew from the refrigerator, readjusted the backpack on my back, and headed for my childhood bedroom.

I opened the door, and my nephews Jackson and Arthur were playing on their phones on my bed. They were the teenagers who were too cool to hang out with the kids.

"Hey guys," I announced myself.

"Sup?" Arthur said, looking up at me for a millisecond. They were most definitely teenagers.

"Good to see you, too. Can you two give me a few minutes so I can set up in here?" I asked.

They grunted but scooted off my bed and out the door. I closed the door behind them. I took a long sip of my cold brew and threw the backpack on the bed.

I looked around at the walls. Nothing in here had changed since last year. I looked over at the posters on my wall. I had a sports section where I pretended to care about certain athletes to get away with posters of shirtless men on my wall. Female pop stars and a shirtless photo of Usher filled my music section. No wonder my mother was not in shock when I came out to her.

I threw myself on my bed and tucked my arm behind my head as I stared at the ceiling. I'm comfortable in this space, in this house. But why does it feel so wrong? Why does it give me anxiety to think about coming here every year?

Quiet is a luxury seldom afforded in this house, especially at Thanksgiving.

The door swung open, and two of my sisters marched in.

"Park, it's so good to see you," Jessica said.

"Did you hear Mandy is pregnant again?" Sun asked.

"Geez. What is she going to do with four babies?" I asked.

"Well, Max got that new job, so they're planning to move to a bigger house in the spring," Sun said.

After a few more rounds of family gossip, it was time to retire to the dinner table. Well, tables. There were so many of us; the main table was connected to a folding table connected to another banquet table Mom borrowed from the church, which was connected to what appeared to be an ironing board.

I sat in the middle of the church table and looked around at the family. My mom was at the head chatting with Mandy. Next to her sat her husband, Max. Her kids cascaded from there. Sun took a seat next to her twin sister, Jessica. Their spouses sat across from them. Their kids were scattered around the table in various spots. Next to me was my youngest sister, Jin. She was flanked by her girlfriend, Rebecca. They had two kids mixed in with Jessica and Sun's kiddos.

The noise in the house was joyous and loud. Jin and I shared a couple of niceties. Sun's husband, Robert, asked for some book recommendations. We all stuffed ourselves with the meal my mother had meticulously cooked for all of us.

After the feast, the powers that be decided we should have a group photo in front of the fireplace. We stuck Mom in the high-backed chair in the middle. Sun grabbed a tripod from somewhere and went to work, positioning everyone in the photo. She grouped Mandy and her family to Mom's right. Jessica and her family were to the left. She positioned Rebecca and Jin together on Mandy's side. Their kids all took a seat in front of them. Robert corralled his kids to Jessica's side and left a hole for Sun after she finished positioning everyone.

Last, and certainly least, was me. I was to be poised on the floor in front of Mom. Alone.

Then it suddenly hit me: being here was uncomfortable. It had nothing to do with anyone in this house and everything to do with me. I was jealous. I wanted what all of my sisters had: a family. I wanted to bring someone home.

My chest got hot, and I fought back tears. I strained my face into the most forced smile I could muster. I remembered what Lea had told me. Grace and space. I've mustered all the grace I could. Right now, I needed space.

7
Ben
1 Year Later

A year had passed since Jeremy's death, and I still wasn't the same. Going to work, meeting deadlines, synergy, and pushing the boundaries of what's possible seemed pointless. Life is unfair. Life is finite. There had to be more to life than this?

I pulled away from everyone. I had seen no mutual friends Jeremy and I shared since the funeral. When tragedy strikes, people don't know what to do. They don't know what to say. So, they ghost. Even Rachel and I grew distant. I still saw her daily, but there wasn't much to say. She came over that night and held me as I wept. It was over a month before I unpacked our vacation bag. It was a solid six months before I could eliminate any of Jeremy's things. Our lease ended, and I decided not to renew. I needed to get out of that space and find a way to move forward. I moved out everything I wanted and hired a crew to donate everything left in the apartment, less the items his family had collected. I was used to grief. I was used to loss. I lost both of my parents before I was twenty.

"Hey you," Rachel popped into my cubicle and took a seat. "I got some tickets to a movie tonight. We're going to see some horrible slasher movie with a completely unbelievable antagonist. We'll stuff ourselves with popcorn and candy and make fun of it the entire time."

"I don't know if—"

"You're coming. It's not negotiable." Rachel knew it was the anniversary of Jeremy's death. I wasn't going to fight her. There would be no point. Doing something stupid, fun, and mindless would be good for me. Probably better than the alternative.

The workday dragged on for what seemed like forever, but finally, the weekend was here. The movie was stupid. The killer was supposed to be a secret, but the writers were not subtle in the early foreshadowing.

"Watch, it's going to be the angry farmer," Rachel whispered.

"You think?" I asked and laughed a little.

"Of course! Those teenagers ran over his dog, and he's going to murder them all in revenge."

That's precisely what happened. They didn't even build up a second possible outcome. They just went with the angry farmer's plan. I never understood why filmmakers made these types of movies. So many good books are out there that never get turned into screenplays. I should become an intermediate agent and pitch people's books to Hollywood. I don't know if that's even a job, but I'm going to make it one.

The movie ended. I thanked Rachel for a great time. I really needed this night.

"I hope I could take your mind off the day at least a little," she said.

"It did. Thank you. It doesn't even feel real because, although the anniversary is today, Thanksgiving isn't until next week this year. It'll probably hit me while I'm spending Thanksgiving alone." I didn't mean for that to sound as desperate as it came out.

"You should join my family for Thanksgiving this year," Rachel blurted, picking up on my desperation. "You know that you're always welcome. Please come."

"I'll think about it," I said, knowing full well I had no intention of going to a house full of strangers with my work friend.

We hugged goodbye, and I went to the parking garage to find my car. It was gone. I was pretty sure I parked on the 4th floor. I wasn't really paying attention. Maybe it was on the 5th. I took the elevator up, and when I exited, an identical floor greeted me, except there were no cars anywhere in sight.

I scanned the aisle where I was confident I had parked and saw a black lump in the middle of the lane. I walked up to the lump carefully, my hand on my phone in my pocket. It looked like a person lying there.

"Hello?" I called out before approaching.

No answer.

I walked closer and could make out hair. It was definitely a person, an elderly person.

"Hello? Are you okay?" I asked louder.

"Oh, thank heavens you're here. Can you help me up?" It was an old woman.

"Of course. Give me your hand."

Extending my arm, I grasped the hand of the elderly woman. I scooted her along until her other arm was accessible enough for her to reach up. I adjusted her to a seated position.

"Alright, ready?" I asked.

"Yep."

I hoisted her to a standing position, and she regained her balance remarkably well.

"Are you okay?" I asked.

"Yes, dear," she said and brushed herself off. "Getting old is a bitch. I don't recommend it."

"I suppose it's better than the alternative," I offered.

"Ha. I suppose you're right," she beamed right at me. She had the kindest, most gentle eyes. She reminded me of my grandmother on my mother's side. This woman had wisdom behind her eyes. I could tell she had seen everything and done it all.

"Do you need me to call someone for you?" I asked.

"No, I'm good now," she said. "It's the push I needed to get myself right. I'll be okay."

"Are you sure?" I asked. "It's no trouble at all."

"No trouble at all," she repeated. "I promise. Now that I'm off that dirty floor, I am good to go."

"Alright, can I walk you downstairs?" I asked.

"Oh no, my car is right over there." She pointed to an old Buick parked nearby.

It was not there when I walked off the elevator. There were no cars up here at all. At least, I didn't think there had been. Now she has me questioning what I saw.

"Alright, I've gotta continue the hunt for my car. I kind of forgot where I've parked," I admitted. "It's lucky that I've mis-parked it. I wouldn't have found you otherwise."

The old woman spun on my words and grabbed me by my arms.

"Luck? What do you know of luck?" she sounded almost angry, for sure upset. "Boy, there is no such thing as luck. It's all about being in the right place at the right time. Don't forget that."

"Okay," I trailed off, stunned and unsure of what to say.

"Go on the trip," she commanded.

"What?" A chill ran down my back.

"Go on the trip you never got to take," she repeated without stuttering.

"What are you saying?" I asked again.

"You need to be at the right place at the right time," she said calmly, as if she didn't just freak out a minute ago. She let go of my arms. She looked deep into my eyes. "You need to be in the right place at the right time. Go on that trip. Be in the right place at the right time."

"Okay," I said, to appease the old woman. I helped her get back to her car. She got in, started the old engine that sputtered to life, and drove out of the parking garage.

Stunned, I stood there at the once-again empty parking garage floor. I turned around and headed back down to the 4th floor. I found my car instantly where I left it.

Too weird. Maybe I'd gone to three the first time by mistake?

Sitting in my car, I thought about what the old woman had said about taking the trip I never got to take. I thought about Coral Cove. I didn't want to take that trip; it had always been Jeremy's dream.

My phone buzzed.

> **Rachel:** Made it home. Please consider joining us for Thanksgiving. I would love to have you.

I stared at the text for a solid minute. I decided to call her and tell her about what had just happened. She didn't even seem phased.

"I think you should go," Rachel said finally.

"I think that's a horrible idea," I said.

"It would offer you much-needed closure," Rachel said. "Why else would the universe have sent you that old woman?"

"The universe didn't send me an old woman. I mis-parked my car and found her."

"You just told me a minute ago that you know your car wasn't there," Rachel said. "Take the sign and go to Coral Cove. Book yourself a nice hotel. NOT the one you were going to go to. Grab some lotion and rent yourself some porn."

Rachel could always make me laugh.

"Alright, bish. I'll see you on Monday."

We hung up, and I thought about my encounter the entire drive home. The words the old lady left me with repeated in my mind. Be in the right place at the right time.

8
Park

"Here we are again, the week of Thanksgiving, and I am nowhere close to being able to bring someone home to meet the family," I whined to Lea.

"You never know. Holidays are magical. They have the power to change your entire life," Lea said.

"Yeah, yeah, yeah. Just because you met Alex at Christmas time doesn't make all holidays magical," I scoffed.

"All I'm saying is that if you keep an open mind and heart, wonderful things can happen."

"You seem to forget I worked with you before you met Alex. You weren't open-minded, and your heart was closed tighter than a vacuum seal," I had to remind her.

"You make me sound like a monster," Lea laughed. "I just want the same magic for you."

"I appreciate you," I said.

I grabbed the stack of new books I just cataloged and headed towards the aisles to put them away. The top book was a young adult fantasy novel about a girl who discovers she's a dragon slayer. I haven't read it, and the reviews have been mixed.

The next book in the stack was an LGBT title by Alaric Valentine, with a very handsome man on the cover. He was shirtless, with rippling abs. His arm was up over his head, exposing a hairy armpit. Gays love them some armpits.

I flipped over the book to read the back. It was a cheesy romance novel about a straight football player who gets seduced by the nerdy but handsome chess champion. I thumbed through the pages and read a section about a steamy shower scene where the chess champion stumbles into the locker room after the big game. It looked terrible. I have never heard of the author. I flipped back to the cover of the shirtless football player. Ugh, where do they find these models? I couldn't believe the filth that gets published.

I pulled out my phone and took a picture of the cover. I will buy this on payday and hate every minute of the guilty pleasure.

I looked at the back again, and this time at the price. Ten dollars. A steal. Nice.

I grinned and placed the book on the shelf, blowing a kiss at the shirtless football player.

"I saw that," a voice said.

Startled, I dropped the rest of the books I was carrying. They made a loud, thunderous noise.

A few seconds later, I heard Lea running towards me. She stopped shy of ten feet away. She looked at me and the handsome stranger who appeared out of nowhere. He was as gorgeous as the football player on the cover.

"Are you okay?" Lea asked. Clearly, she was reliving the events of last year.

"He's okay. I scared him, that's all," the handsome stranger said. He bent down to pick up the books off the ground. I reached down to help him.

I looked up at Lea and said, "I'm good. No crashes this time."

Lea looked the guy up and down while his attention was on the books. She silently gave me a nod and an "okay" sign with her fingers. Then she casually strolled away.

"What happened last year?" the handsome stranger asked.

"I uh..." There was no use lying or trying to figure a way out of this question. "I fell. I reached for a couple of books on the top shelf, and the shelf gave out and knocked about two rows on top of me."

"Yikes. You should have used a ladder." He had such kind eyes. He had immaculately coiffed hair, a beautiful stark chin, and kissable lips.

"Yes, I should have. Lea gave me an earful."

"Ha. And that was a year ago today, huh?" he asked.

"Well, kind of. It was Thanksgiving week. I remember because I was distracted about visiting my family," I said with immediate regret. I can't believe I was opening up this much to a perfect stranger.

He smiled, and I was able to take a pause and look him up and down. He was an impeccable dresser with broad shoulders, spindly arms underneath his tight ribbed sweater, and thick, juicy thighs.

"Thanksgiving wasn't great for me last year either," he admitted.

"Oh? What happened?" I asked.

"I don't really want to talk about it if that's okay?" he said.

"Yeah, of course." I turned away and then turned back towards him. I wasn't sure what to do or say now. Taking the books from his hands, I turned to refile.

As I grabbed the books, my hand brushed up against his stomach. It has been too long since I've had a rushing feeling.

It was intoxicating.

His cologne wafted over me, and I could feel myself engorge. I lowered the books, hoping he wouldn't notice.

He's a man; he noticed instantly.

"What have you got going on down there?" he smirked.

I felt hot and flush. I didn't know what to say.

"It's okay, I think you're adorable," he said.

Instantly, I felt more at ease. He's at least not married to a woman this time around. That's a step in the right direction. Gods, what to do next? I needed to get these books re-shelved, but a hot gay dude who is clearly into me never happens.

Lea would understand.

I shot my shot.

Setting the books down on a free shelf, I turned to give him my full attention. I leaned casually on the bookshelf, forgetting about the tent building in my pants.

"What brings you to town?" I asked.

"Is it that obvious I'm a tourist?" he smiled.

I melted. "Well, it's a small town. We know just about everyone. I would have noticed you." I grinned.

"I arrived last night." I got a nice seafront hotel room up the road and came to check out the local shops. This place drew me in as I am a huge fan of books.

"How long are you in town?" I asked.

"The weekend."

"Are you alone?"

"I am."

"Well, this may be forward, but can I buy you dinner tonight?" I asked.

"Wow. Just going for it, huh?" He leaned in closer. The smell of his cologne sent a tingle up my spine.

"I believe in the magic of the holidays." I can't believe I said it. Lea would be so proud. "What kind of food do you like?"

"I'm not picky," he said.

"So, is that a yes?" I asked.

He chuckled. "Do I get to know your name first?"

I am an idiot.

"Sorry," I laughed and covered my face. "I'm Park."

I reached out my hand to shake his. He raised a perfectly manicured hand and wrapped it around mine. I felt a wave of shivers. I've never felt such soft hands. A glowing, hot sensation tickled my stomach like a million butterflies. I wanted to pull him into me. I resisted and instead shook up and down twice and let go.

"Nice to meet you, Park. What time do you get off?" he asked.

I looked at my watch. It was almost three pm, and I was scheduled to close. I usually got out of here around nine pm. I needed to take this man to dinner.

"Uh, I think I'm off in a couple of hours, actually," I lied.

"Alright, well, should we meet at six somewhere for an early dinner?" he asked.

"Yes! Do you like Chinese?" I asked.

"Love it."

"We have an amazing Chinese restaurant that we love just a couple of blocks away," I point towards the restaurant. "Meet me there at six?"

"It's a date," he says.

We walk together towards the door.

"I really feel it's my duty as a faithful Coral Covian to make sure that everyone in town has the best experience they can while they're here." I don't know why I said this.

"Oh yeah? I thought it was because you thought I was sexy," he said.

"Well, that does factor into it," I said. "I just really believe in being hospitable."

He leaned in, got close to my ear, and whispered, "Judging by the bulge in your pants, I'd say it was a pretty large factor." He backed away and winked at me as he exited the door.

I stood there, my mouth agape, as I watched him stroll down the street and out of sight. After I could no longer see him, I turned and ran for the register.

"Oh my god, oh my god, oh my god," I screamed at Lea.

"What a fox!" she said. She was grinning from ear to ear. "Please tell me you got his phone number."

"No."

Her shoulders sunk.

"No, but we are meeting at six for dinner at the Chinese restaurant," I said, realizing I blurted that out before asking if she could cover for me.

"At six, huh?" She smirked. Nothing gets past Lea.

"Yeah," I grimaced, "Are you okay with covering for me tonight?"

"Park," she grabbed my shoulders, "it would be my honor."

"Thank you, thank you, thank you." I gave her a tight hug.

"So, dish! What happened? I could barely see you from over here."

I retold her the events. Kissing the cover model (she laughed out loud), him smelling like a god-damn angel (she agreed she smelled his cologne when she came to check on me), and I even told her the part about me getting a boner and what he whispered in my ear.

"That is fucking hot," Lea said.

"I know!"

"You should get out of here now. Go home, change, wear something sexy," Lea suggested.

"You think?"

"You can't show up in your work clothes," she scoffed.

"You're right," I admitted. "Alright, I'm getting out of here."

I grabbed my backpack and keys out of the upstairs office. I handed her the scanner from my back pocket and headed out the door.

"Wait," she called after me.

I stopped and turned back.

"What was his name?"

"Fuck!"

9
Ben

I booked my flights the following day. I slept on the decision. It was the first time since the accident that I had dreamed of Jeremy. I don't remember the details of the dream, but I woke up feeling at peace. I know he would want me to take this trip.

I texted Rachel about my decision. She was supportive of the idea. We texted a few hotel options back and forth and picked one. I sent her my itinerary, and she researched some local sites for me to visit.

I told my boss I was taking a few extra days off. He seemed happy that I was finally taking some time for myself.

It was a pleasant flight to Coral Cove. The rental car experience was smoother than I have ever experienced. The time from check-in to my driving away was less than twenty minutes. It almost felt illegal how quickly it went.

While driving to the hotel, I cracked the window and let the fresh air wash over me. Never in my memory have I experienced a dewy sweetness in the air. I've read about it before in books, but here I was sipping it in. I felt instantly calm and at ease in Coral Cove.

It was intoxicating.

The woman at the hotel who checked me in was friendly and welcoming. She asked where I was from and about things I'd like to see while in town, and she even gave me coupons for businesses around town. It would have felt creepy anywhere else, but in Coral Cove, it felt different.

In my room, I opened the sliding door to the balcony and drank in more of the sea air.

I walked around the central part of town as darkness fell. It was getting late. Most of the shops were shutting down. String lights crisscrossed the street, giving the entire street a warm glow. I had dinner at a cute little café recommended by the woman at the hotel. I used a twenty-five percent off coupon, too.

Up ahead, I saw a sign for a bookstore, Spellbound Stories. I approached the door and noticed it was closing in fifteen minutes. I didn't want to be that guy. Never have I ever spent just fifteen minutes in a bookstore.

I peeked in from the windows and looked at all the goodies. It was fantasy-themed and an absolute gem. I saw their romance section, their LGBT section—which was nice to see in a small town—and my favorite historical fiction section. There was a magical fantasy element in the whole place. I would come back the next day and spend a couple of hours here.

I looked towards the front register and saw the cutest guy I'd ever seen working behind the desk. He was checking out a customer and was clearly talking about what they were buying. He looked so passionate about his books. It made me smile.

I looked down at his chest; he was wearing a thin t-shirt, and his nipples were protruding through. I could feel myself get stiff.

He had a very distinct and strong jawline. I'm a sucker for a good jawline. He had a muscly but thin neck. I imagined myself kissing his neck.

I would most definitely be coming back tomorrow.

Back at the hotel, I thanked the front desk lady for the dinner recommendation. I told her I was excited to explore more of the town.

Inside my room, I stripped down to my boxers and pulled out my cell phone. I flew onto the bed, onto my stomach, and shoved a pillow under my chest.

> **Me:** There is something magical about this town.

A minute later, Rachel texted back.

> **Rachel:** Oh yeah? Tell me about it.

I tried my best to describe the air, the seaside calmness, and the charming hospitality of the town without sounding like a flaming homosexual. I was unsuccessful.

> **Rachel:** I think that sounds like you're exactly where you need to be right now. Enjoy it. Text me tomorrow.

I promised her I would.

While lying on my back, thoughts of the handsome guy from the bookstore filled my mind. While contemplating his jawline, neck, and pecs, I reached down and stroked myself over my underwear. I was hard. I imagined stripping off his shirt and kissing his neck and chest.

I reached inside my underwear and started stroking myself. I realized I hadn't masturbated in a long time. It felt amazing. The tingles shot to my toes, curling uncontrollably.

I imagined grabbing that guy by the back of the neck and pulling his mouth to mine. Apparently, that was all it took before shivers exploded from within.

Carefully, I scooted to the edge of my bed and duck-walked into the bathroom to clean myself off. I climbed back into bed and was asleep before I knew it.

The following day, I took my time getting out of bed and showered. I grabbed breakfast from the hotel lobby, a coffee and a bagel. Nothing to write home about, but they would suffice.

We dedicated a good part of the day to walking the beach, heading back to the main street, checking out a few shops here and there, heading back out to the beach, and strolling along the piers. I was taking everything in sip by sip.

Musicians and artists lined the streets and piers. I stopped often, listening to their music, or admired their paintings. There was an old guy selling beach glass jewelry. A small charm with a daisy caught my eye. I bought it for Rachel.

After lunch, I stopped by the bookstore and spent the afternoon getting lost in the aisles.

When I entered the shop, I saw a lady behind the counter.

Shoot.

Maybe he wasn't here today. I scanned around but didn't see him anywhere.

"Welcome. Please, have a look around, and if you need help with anything, let me know," the woman smiled.

"Thank you," I said and nodded. I headed directly toward the historical fiction and dove in. I flipped through title after title. She had a fantastic collection. I was surprised by how many of these books I hadn't read yet.

Time had no meaning inside that bookstore, and I couldn't tell you how long I was staring at the books. Behind me, I heard a voice talking with the woman at the front.

It was the guy!

I sank behind a row of books where I could peer out like a pervert in the bushes. I laughed at myself for the comparison.

The two were talking about some book that had just come in. It was evident that he had a love for books. His smile melted me. His shirt today was thicker, and I couldn't see his nipples.

He turned away from me, and I got my first glimpse of his ass. What a perfect bubble butt. I scanned my way down his tight pants and saw some beautiful, thick calves. Another of my weaknesses is a nice set of calves. My pants got tighter.

I needed to walk away. The comparison between me and the pervert in the bush was becoming too apt.

I moved back towards the LGBT section and started perusing the titles. I recognized quite a few of the books. They carried all the most popular ones. I selected a colorful book that caught my eye at the end and started flipping through the pages. It seemed like a quick read. I was looking for something with more substance.

Out of the corner of my eye, I saw the handsome sales guy walking towards me. I waved like an idiot, but thankfully, he didn't see me.

He was examining some book with a shirtless hunk on the cover.

Score! He's queer.

I smiled to myself. He turned the book over to read the back. I watched in silence. He turned the book over again and set it on the shelf. He snapped a photo of the book. Then he blew the book a kiss.

What a cutie.

"I saw that," I said.

He dropped the books, and all the blood rushed out of his face.

The manager ran over, and I assured her it was my fault. The next thing I knew, he was asking me out. I couldn't believe my luck.

Luck. I suddenly thought of the woman in the parking garage.

Maybe this wasn't luck, like the lady said. Perhaps I was exactly where I needed to be.

"Park," I said, rolling his name over my tongue once outside the bookstore. "A cute name for a cute guy."

I walked down the street and noted the Chinese restaurant where I had agreed to meet him. I picked up speed and rushed back to the hotel to change before meeting him again.

Me: I have a date.

Rachel: What? That's amazing!! I want all the

details. Be safe and have
fun!

She also sent many smiley face emojis. I didn't
know you could send that many in a row. After getting
ready, I looked at the clock; it was five-thirty, and I had
half an hour to walk ten minutes.

Nothing wrong with being early.

I arrived at the Chinese restaurant and glanced
around the space. It was small, and I could see every
table from the front. Park was nowhere to be found.
Not unsurprisingly, I was nearly twenty minutes early.

"Table for one?" asked the host.

I smiled and met their eyes. "Not tonight. Table for
two, please."

10
Park

"Hello, handsome," I said, playing it cool as I joined my mystery date at the table he got for us.

"Park!" He smiled up at me. He stood up from his seat and embraced me in a warm hug. "Thank you for taking me out."

"It's my pleasure. I hope I didn't keep you waiting," I checked my watch. There were still five minutes left until six. "I said six pm, right?"

"Yes. I guess I was excited to see you again and got here about twenty minutes early," he shot me a cheeky smile.

My knees quivered. I sat down quickly to combat the weakness.

We ordered our meals and slipped into easy conversation. I couldn't believe how much we had in common. We both had a love for a rare anime series that none of my friends had ever heard of.

It shocked me that he had known them.

He told me about his job, feeling lost in his position. "Everything is deadlines and more than the day before.

I'm ready for a change. I think I'm at this place in my life where I want—need things to be different. Slower maybe? You know?"

"I completely understand. When I worked for a giant conglomerate, I had a similar experience. I was in full burnout and came here on a mini vacation. I changed my whole life overnight by quitting the big times and moving to Coral Cove. It's still the best decision I ever made," I smiled.

"It looks good on you," he teased.

"Thanks," I said, blushing.

The waitress came by to take our order. "Hey, Park, what can I get you two?"

I nodded to my date, and he ordered first.

"I'll have the General Tsao's chicken with white rice," he said.

I couldn't contain the bubbling laughter.

"Your usual, Park?" the waitress asked.

"Yes, please," I smiled. "Can I also get an iced tea?"

"Oh, I'll have one of those, too," my date said.

"Sure thing!" the waitress said before skipping away. When she returned, it was with two orders of General Tsao's and white rice.

"Your regular order is my regular order?" his smile was striking. All the way to his eyes.

I shrugged. "I can't help it. It's the best thing on the menu."

The hours flew by, and before I knew it, we were the only two left in the restaurant. May, the owner, came over and gently told me she wanted to close up.

"Shall we continue this evening with a walk on the beach? I think it's a full moon tonight. I bet it's gorgeous," I suggested.

"Yes, please," he said.

I paid the bill with May, and we walked out into the street.

His arm bumped up against mine. His hand tapped my wrist gently, testing the waters. He slipped his fingers between mine, and I let him take my hand.

Yum, those soft hands again. I wanted to turn and melt right into him. We walked hand in hand down the street and turned at my favorite beach entrance at the Union Wharf. I pulled him down the alleyway.

I stopped abruptly and pulled him close as I backed into a building.

"I have to admit something," I said.

"Oh? What?"

"I still don't know your name," I grimaced.

"Oh, my gods," he laughed, covering his face. "I can't believe we've been together for hours, and I haven't told you my name. I'm Ben. Ben Dawson."

I reached out my hand to shake his. He gave me his, and I didn't let him go. I pulled his face close to mine.

"It's very nice to meet you, Ben." I moved in ninety percent of the way.

He met me the last ten, and we kissed. It started out with a gentle peck, but passion took over. Ben pressed into me, and our mouths opened slowly. His tongue gently stroked my lips as we made out.

Ben pinned me against the building with his body. He pressed into me. His hands explored my chest over the top of my sweatshirt. Our kissing grew more intense.

Our breathing more rhythmic.

Our tongues intertwined, and my hands rubbed up his back. I could feel the dip in the small of his back and worked my hands up his spine towards the back of his head. I grabbed him by the nape, and he let out a guttural grunt.

Ben backed away a few inches. "Sorry about that. Necks are my biggest turn-on, and grabbing me like that set off something primal in me."

"Never apologize for that." I grabbed his head and pulled him back into mine. More brazenly, I ran my hand down his back towards his ass. Testing the waters, I rubbed the upper part of his left cheek.

He pulled away a few inches again and snapped his teeth. "Rrrarrr. Park, you are feeling a bit frisky?"

I smiled. "Absolutely."

He reached around and grabbed my hand from his ass and pulled me back around.

"Which way is the beach?" he asked.

"This way," I pointed.

I didn't want to stop kissing this beautiful man. I hope I haven't pushed it too far. He clasped my hand tighter as we walked down to the moonlit beach.

We found a large piece of driftwood, sat beside each other, watched the waves crash, and talked. We talked about family and how he had always wanted a large family but lost his parents at an early age. He had no siblings.

I told him about my gigantic family and all my siblings, their spouses, and my nieces and nephews. He wanted to hear about each of them. He listened patiently as I covered every member of my family.

He just smiled and listened.

He listened.

"I'm sorry to be yakking your ear off about my gigantic family and their drama," I said.

Ben didn't answer. He just leaned in and kissed me some more. Our tongues wrestling back and forth. This time, his hands were exploring my back. He tugged at the t-shirt tucked into my pants, pulling it out. His hand went up my bare back.

Shivers electrified my entire body. I wanted more. I reached over to put my hand under the front of his shirt. Instead, I brushed up against his rock-hard penis.

I pulled back.

"Oh, my gods, I'm sorry," I said. "I didn't mean to be that forward."

"Did you like what you felt?" he said with a crooked smile.

"Absolutely."

"Do you want to come back to my hotel room?" he asked.

"Absolutely."

11

Ben

I can't believe I met this man a few hours ago and am already bringing him back to my hotel room. But when it feels right, it feels right.

The passion between us ignited faster in my hotel room than on the beach. I barely let Park get his shoes off before I was lifting his shirt above his head.

I took a half step back to take him in.

Fuck, he was beautiful.

Park's jawline led me to a thin, sturdy neck tucked neatly into a sharp V of his clavicle. His chest was smooth and firm. His nipples were erect and absolutely perfect.

Reaching up, I gently played with his left nipple, pinching it between two fingers. Park moaned, and I couldn't help myself. I pulled him into me and used both of my hands to explore his back.

Running my hands up and down from his neck to his waistline, I reached to his nape and gave a gentle but firm squeeze. He let out a moan, and my dick stiffened even more. With my left hand, I dragged my fingers along his waistband and dipped them below his pants.

He thrust into me, our crotches merging for the first time.

A moan escaped both of us. I took this as a green light and slid my entire hand down the back of his pants. I grabbed hold of his ass and squeezed. My other hand joined with his other cheek.

With both of my hands down his pants, his pants were extra tight. I decided it was best if I helped him with this new problem.

I slipped my hands partially out of the back of his pants and glided them around the front, all the while keeping my hands inside. I made my way to the front of his pants and undid his button.

I paused momentarily, looking for an okay to continue while allowing him to tell me no.

He kissed me harder.

I unzipped his pants and let my hand drag across the front of his boxer briefs. I stopped kissing him long enough so I could pull his pants down. My hands gently caressed his cock on the way back up to his mouth.

I felt his cock pulse.

We continued making out until I shoved him backward onto the bed and climbed on top of him. He reached down to my waist and pulled my shirt over my head. He rubbed his right hand down the middle of my chest, caressing my patch of chest hair.

"You like that?" I asked him.

"Fucking love it," he growled and closed his fist on my chest hair and gently tugged at it.

Another primal groan escaped me. No one had ever pulled on my chest hair like that.

It drove me crazy.

I laid down flat on top of him, letting our chests rub together. I started thrusting into him. Our cocks rubbed together between too many layers of fabric.

"How about we get you out of those jeans?" he asked.

I flipped off of him, and we lay side by side on our backs as I unbuttoned and unzipped my pants. I wiggled out of my jeans and kicked them onto the floor. We continued lying side by side, and I stared into his eyes.

We said nothing.

Park lifted my hand, rubbing the back of it along with my knuckles.

He leaned into me and gave me another kiss.

"You are beautiful," he whispered.

"So are you," I said.

I climbed back on top of him. This time, only our thin layers of underwear separated our throbbing cocks. A wet spot appeared at the top of his underwear. I let my fingers slip down and played with the wet spot.

"That's a lot of precum," I said.

"What can I say? You turn me on," he said.

I couldn't take any more teasing; I had to taste him. My body slid down his. Taking my time to caress his neck and his chest, to kiss and gently nibble on his nipples. He squirmed and moaned as I teased his nipple. I made my way back to the middle of his chest and started kissing my way south. I stopped briefly at his belly button, licking my way around it.

I continued south and kissed the top of his penis through his underwear. The sweetness of his precum lingered on my lips and tongue.

I let out a primal moan again. I raised my hands to his waistband, grabbed ahold of each side of his underwear, and tugged down gently, revealing all of him to me.

I took him all in. My mouth filled with his ample appendage.

Thrusting back and forth, his back arched, and he squirmed and moaned. I reached my hands back up his chest toward his nipples, all the while keeping him locked inside of my mouth. I gently pinched his nipple, and he squirmed around even more.

I released him from my mouth momentarily and began licking along the side down to his balls. My tongue explored him up and down and up and down again. I returned to the tip and took him once more.

He arched again, and I supported his back with my free hand to keep him locked in the arch position. My other hand focused on his chest and nipples while keeping him locked inside. He moaned faster and faster, and I could feel him quiver and shake inside of me.

He squealed and unloaded in my mouth. He tried to pull away, but I drank him in. I let his sweetness fill my mouth, and I swallowed him down.

Gently, I pulled my lips away from his body and wiped my face.

"That was delicious," I said.

"Oh my god, that felt amazing," Park said, pulling me in for a kiss. His tongue explored my mouth. The same mouth he just filled.

We fell together in an embrace, and it wasn't long before we were asleep, with me holding him. It felt amazing.

I was supposed to find this boy today.

12

Park

The sun glowed through the cracked blinds. It took me a moment to remember where I was. Across my middle was the arm of one of the sweetest men I'd ever met. I rolled over onto my back, and Ben readjusted and laid his head on my chest. With my free arm, I raised up and stroked his hair.

It felt amazing to sleep with someone. I tried to remember the last time I had shared a bed with a guy and came up short. I wanted this moment to last forever.

Then it hit me. It's Thanksgiving.

"Fuck," I whispered and jolted slightly.

The jolt was gentle, but enough to disturb Ben. He shuffled awake.

"What's up?" he said in a half yawn.

"Sorry, didn't mean to wake you," I said. "I forgot that today is Thanksgiving, and I'm supposed to head to my mom's house."

"Oh, shit." Ben pulled himself from my chest and rose. I grabbed him and pulled him back into me.

"No, don't leave. There's nowhere I'd rather be than right here, right now. With you."

"Awww," Ben rolled over to look into my eyes, but was still half on top of me. "But you can't miss Thanksgiving with your family. That's not right."

"I don't want this to end," I admitted.

"Me either, but I can't allow you to miss family time. That would be so selfish of me," Ben said with a smile.

We lay in bed for another fifteen minutes or so, just being near each other. My hands traced lines on his body. I ran my fingers through his chest hair, driving him wild.

My hand slipped down his stomach to a tiny happy trail of hair that went from his navel down under his boxer briefs.

"It's my turn to explore," I said, rolling onto my side, still nude from the night before. I tugged at his underwear until they were down around his ankles. I moved my way back to his cock and stroked it, gently admiring its size and girth.

I stroked my two fingers at the top, rolling his foreskin back and forth, making him wiggle and squirm in delight. I cupped his balls with one hand and gently massaged while kissing gently at his tip.

I teased a little longer before giving in and taking him into my mouth. Slowly, at first, feeling every inch swell into my palate. I pulled my other free hand to make a fist right before my mouth. I let go of a ton of saliva and let it drip into my palm.

With a thoroughly damp grip, my mouth and palm worked in fervor tandem.

Faster and faster.

Ben's body squirmed in pleasure, his back arching off the mattress.

He was just about to release when I got an idea.

"Wait," I stopped mid-stroke. "I have a crazy idea."

"What? Why? Huh?"

I just did a very mean thing.

"Why don't you come with me to my mom's?" I asked.

"Really? You stopped to ask me that right now?" he laughed.

Thank gods, he laughed. I bet people have been killed for less.

"Please?" I asked.

"I mean, I don't have any other plans," he said. "You're sure it won't be a problem?"

"No. I told you about how large my family is. Another person will not make or break the food situation."

Ben just laughed at me and shook his head. He sat up, grabbed me by my neck and shoulders, and pulled me into a kiss. I fell back onto the bed with him.

"It's kind of a long drive. Five hours kind of long," I said, looking away.

"I see. You were waiting for me to answer before you dropped that bombshell on me." Ben smiled.

"No," I said, feeling mortified. "No, I swear it wasn't like that. I was just enjoying myself so much, but I tend to overthink things all the time, even when I'm in the midst of doing," I pointed to his crotch, "...that."

Ben rolled over and grabbed his phone. I got a glimpse of his bare, beautiful ass for the first time. It was impossible for me to resist. I lunged at it and gave it a tiny bite. He squealed, and we both laughed.

"Five hours probably means we should get going soon," he said.

"After I finish up here." I traveled back down to his cock.

"No, no. I don't want a rush job. Let's finish that later. For now, let's get in the shower and get ready. Don't want to keep mom waiting."

Even though he was now standing next to the bed completely naked, the fact he was worried about disappointing my family made him extremely sexy to me.

We showered quickly, especially for gay men. I told him to pack a bag for an overnight. He was all right with that added surprise as well. We popped into his rental car and drove to my house, where I ran inside quickly, gathered a few things to fill my overnight bag, and switched vehicles to mine.

On the drive up, we continued to chat. We learned we are both dog people. I love Great Danes, and he loves German Shepherds, though neither of us feels like we have the time for a puppy right now.

He wants to own a bed-and-breakfast someday. It's not an Airbnb but a legit bed-and-breakfast with at least six rooms. He would wake up and cook a full English breakfast, his favorite meal.

I told him about Lea and the bookstore and how she's not just my boss, but also my best friend. He told me about Rachel, and she sounded lovely. During the drive, he sent her a few text messages. He didn't text her last night because of being otherwise occupied. She was worried.

I wondered what she thought about me stealing him away for Thanksgiving, but I didn't ask. I'm already moving fast with this boy.

Despite being five hours long, the drive flew by, with Ben by my side. I'd never felt so instantly connected to someone.

My hand rested on the shifter as I drove the highways toward my mother's house. Ben reached down and glided his hand along the back of mine and pulled it off the shifter, holding my hand.

I smiled at him. It felt all too right.

We arrived at my mom's house. My heart started pounding out of my chest. I realized I had notified no one I would bring a guest.

Not that permission would have been required, but I suppose a small notice would have probably been appropriate.

My sisters are going to attack him.

Mom will be polite.

"I hope you're ready for this," I said, pulling into the driveway. I let go of his hand to put the vehicle in park and press the ignition button to turn it off.

"What am I getting myself into?" Ben didn't look worried at all.

"The confidence is extremely sexy," I said.

We exited my car, and I grabbed our bags. I handed him his. He got his backpack situated. I grabbed his hand, and we made our way inside.

"Ooooooh, Park has a booooooooy with him," Sun shouted almost immediately as we walked into the house.

Chaos erupted.

"Here we go," I whispered to Ben.

The typical swirl of hugs and greetings seemed to never end with the mass of sisters, spouses, nieces, and nephews. In the thick of it all, I lost track of Ben. He was not in the living room and not in the dining room. He wasn't in the family room downstairs.

I ran to my bedroom, not expecting him to be there, but unsure where else he'd be. I threw down my bag and continued my hunt. No one was in the bathroom.

Into the kitchen, and there he was, chatting with my mother. They hadn't seen me yet, so I leaned against the door frame and watched.

"Oh, I am so happy you could join us, Ben," my mom said.

"Thank you so much for having me. I'm sorry that Park didn't tell you I was coming ahead of time," Ben said.

"Not at all. The surprise delights us. I am happy to see Park with someone. Someone so handsome, too, is an added bonus," she tapped him on the shoulder.

Ben blushed and then caught me staring from the door frame. He smiled. "Can I help you with something in here?"

"Absolutely not. You go find Park, tell him to hug his mother, and then you boys have fun until dinner. I hope you're staying the night?" she gave him a gentle shove.

It was time for me to rescue him.

"Hello, mama." I reached for my mom and wrapped her in a hug.

She pulled me down to whisper in my ear, "He is so cute."

"Don't I know it," I smiled. "Alright, we'll get out of your hair. I'm going to show him to my room. Love you, see you at dinner."

I grabbed Ben by the arm and dragged him down the hallway to my bedroom. We got shoved to the side by a few of the nephews running by. I looked back at Ben, and he had survived.

We ducked into my childhood bedroom and closed the door.

"Are you alright?" I asked him.

13
Ben

Rachel: You're going to his parents' house the day after meeting him?

Rachel was right to be suspicious.

Me: I'm telling you. This feels so right, and what's the harm? We'll go and have dinner.

Rachel: You could be murdered.

Me: Well, then, it was just my time.

I laughed to myself.

"What's so funny?" Ben asked. I don't think he noticed I was texting because he was still driving us to his mom's house.

"Oh, I just told Rachel that we're doing this. She thinks I'm crazy, and you're going to end up being a murderer." I laughed.

"You never know. She could be right," Park chuckled.

Gods, I love his laugh, and I love making him laugh.

I looked down and saw his right hand on the shifter and took it to hold him for the remainder of the drive.

As we pulled into the driveway, I got an almost déjà vu feeling that I had been here before. Park grabbed our bags from the back and handed me mine.

"I hope you're ready for this," Park said as he smirked a Cheshire grin.

I should be nervous, but I'm not. It just feels right with him. "What am I getting myself into?" I tried to match his smile.

"The confidence is extremely sexy."

Hand in hand, we marched inside. As soon as I entered, the largest family I had ever experienced surrounded me. It was loud, chaotic, and hectic, and it was the most beautiful thing on the face of the Earth. Kids everywhere are excited to meet me and ask me my name.

Where did I come from?

What do you do?

What's your favorite food?

They were eager to hear everything about me.

I was pulled away from Park by a sister. I think she said her name was Jessica. She told me I needed to meet Mom immediately.

Maybe Park should be here for this, but I just went with the flow.

"Mom, this is Ben, a boy that Park brought here," Jessica said.

"Park brought a boy?" she looked up at me. "Oooh, such a nice-looking one, too. Welcome, you can call me Mom." She came in for a hug straight away.

It has been so long since I have had a mom hug that I probably lingered too long with it, but if she noticed, she didn't say anything. She stayed tight until I let up.

"So, where are you from?" Mom asked.

"Originally from Atlanta, but now I am in New York," I said.

"How long have you known my Park?" she asked.

I was kind of dreading this question from everyone. "Not long at all, actually," I admitted, intentionally vague with the details.

"That's okay. It's not about how long you are together. It's more about the quality of the time you spend together."

I couldn't think of a better response. I have had more quality connection with Park than anyone in such a long time.

Park showed up and guided me to his childhood bedroom. I scanned the walls and noted all the pop stars and shirtless boys.

He asked me if I was okay. I wondered what it was on my face that gave me away.

"I need to tell you something," I admitted.

"Okay," Park said.

I sat on his bed and patted the spot next to me to signal he should sit down.

"I want to be open and honest with you. Completely," I said.

There was fear in his eyes.

"I want to tell you why I was in Coral Cove," I said.

Before I knew it, I word-vomited the entire story to him. Everything about Jeremy. The proposal. I even told him about the old woman in the parking garage.

I cried.

He cried.

Park wiped away my tears and looked me straight in the eyes. "Every little thing is just the stepping stones that brought you to me. Thank you for telling everything. Now I owe you something."

He stood up off the bed and walked over to the door. Turning the knob, he locked it. Park turned back to me with a devilish grin. "Let's get those pants off of you," he said.

Before I knew it, he pulled me to stand beside his bed. He pulled my shirt up and over my head so fast that by the time I realized what was happening, he was already at my waist, undoing my button.

He wasted no time and pulled my boxer briefs off with my pants. Now, completely nude, less my socks, he thrust me backward onto his bed. I bounced a couple of times. As soon as I was settled, he kissed my thighs, sending a bolt of pleasure up and down my spine.

He took all my soft cock into his mouth and rubbed it side to side with his tongue. It took no time for me to get fully erect inside of his mouth.

He ravished me like he was on death row, and my meat was his last meal. He got his hands involved and applied pressure under my ball sack, which made me even harder.

Never fully letting me go from his mouth, he managed to send spit down to his fingers. He drooled down the shaft until it dripped down to my anus. I felt his cool fingers gliding past my hole.

He kept sliding the skin of my shaft up and down with his wet fist in one hand, taking it all in his mouth and fondling my hole with his other. Pleasure utterly consumed and wholly enveloped me.

My eyes rolled back in my head, and I thrust and flailed around uncontrollably on his bed. I moaned out loud. Caught myself and threw a hand over my mouth.

Park stopped and looked up from my midsection. "Nobody is going to hear you over the clamoring out there. I want you to moan as loud as you fucking want," he said with the firmest tone I'd ever heard from him.

That set off the primal side in me. I looked down at Park as his face bounced up and down on my cock. I reached down and ran my fingers through his hair.

Up and down.

Up and down.

I grabbed his nape and gave him a gentle shove, forcing him to take all of me. He took it like a champ. I held him there, and it felt amazing.

Water welled in his eyes, and I released him. He pulled back, but not all the way off.

"Look at me," I commanded.

Park looked up at me with his sweet eyes, mouth full of my cock.

"Good boy," I said.

14
Park

I have never in my life had someone say "good boy" to me like that in the middle of sex. My gods, when I tell you, everything in my whole body shook to the core.

It made me suck him harder and deeper. I wanted to pull him so close to me he could never let me go.

I played with his hole, listening to him moan. I could tell he was still stifling his pleasure a little, but at least he was letting it out.

"Get up here," he commanded.

I obeyed.

Ben slipped my shirt off me as I leaned over him. He then pulled me in for a kiss, my mouth still hot from his package.

He rolled me over and undid my pants. Following that, he removed my boxer briefs. Ben grabbed my cock and played with it for a few seconds. I was hard as a rock and ready before he unwrapped me.

He met my mouth with his, and we kissed again, dripping with each other's wetness.

"I want you to fuck me," Ben said.

"Yes, sir," I replied. I pulled my jeans over to me and grabbed a condom from the pocket. I rolled it over my cock and met his mouth again for another kiss.

I shoved Ben to his back. I kissed his neck.

Ben let out a loud noise that was half moan and half squeal. He didn't try to hide it.

This set me ablaze.

I followed his body down slowly, kissing his clavicle, his pecs, and his nipples one at a time. I breathed deeply into his armpit. It smelled like a mixture of cologne and man.

I let out a growl. Continuing southward, I licked his armpit. I followed the curves of his abs down to his throbbing cock. I gave it a few more thrusts in my mouth before grabbing his thick thighs and tossing them into the air, exposing his hole to me.

I started gently and spit at his hole. I started with one finger.

Ben moaned in approval.

I added another finger, moving in and out. His breathing picked up.

After a moment, I added a third finger. This time, curling them while inside of him.

Ben's moaning increased.

Fuck, I was so hard.

"Are you ready for me?" I asked.

"Fuck yes," he said.

Harvesting Love

I entered him slowly at first and watched his eyes roll back. He breathed through my insertion like a good boy. My thrusts were slow and steady.

He felt so warm and tight. I didn't know how long I could keep myself from exploding. I slowed down to give myself some time. I wanted to be in this moment forever.

The moaning never subsided, and Ben was breathing heavily.

I picked up speed.

Slamming in and out faster and faster.

We both moaned in tandem.

I felt the tingling sensation inside of me, and I knew I was going to erupt imminently. Another thrust and I screamed out.

So did Ben.

His white cream exploded all over his stomach in a lava-like flow. I continued pulsating for another few seconds after emptying inside of him.

Eventually, the feeling returned to my body, and I could make eye contact with him.

His smile said it all.

I released his hole back to him and laid myself on top of him, making his mess our mess.

I pulled him in for another kiss.

"Ready for dinner?" I asked with a sheepish grin.

"Really?" Ben laughed.

We cleaned ourselves up, found our clothing, and put ourselves together again before heading back out with the family. We took turns darting into the bathroom to wash up a bit more.

At dinner, I looked around at the family. Everyone had chosen their usual spots, and I positioned myself in the center with a clear view of the family. Mom was at the head of the table laughing with Sun about gods only knows what.

Everyone's families all blended and huddled together to form one giant conglomerate. I looked around at everyone, but no one looked back at me. They consumed themselves in eating and their own conversations.

I glanced over at Ben, and for the first time, I genuinely felt I was where I was supposed to be.

With whom I was supposed to be with.

He took a bite of turkey and smiled at me while chewing.

I smiled back.

Ben glanced over at the stuffing bowl in front of Jessica and then looked up at her. "Can you please pass the stuffing?"

"Oh, you didn't get enough earlier?" Jessica said with a laugh.

Everyone heard, and the adults all erupted in laughter. Clearly, we weren't as stealthy as we thought.

After dinner, it was time for the family photo. Sun gathered her tripod and camera and went to work organizing everyone where they belonged.

Harvesting Love

This time, Ben joined me in front of Mom, and we huddled together on the floor.

He put his arms around me.

Lea was right. Holiday magic is a thing.

If you enjoyed *Harvesting Love*, please check out the next title in the Coral Cove series:

Dawning Desire

Lilly

I was betrothed.

I was never supposed to fall in love with beauty as radiant as the moonlight itself.

But we fell in love anyway.

The gods cursed my love to live as a human for ten-thousand years.

She forgets who I am over and over and over.

So, I have to reminder her.

Ophelia

She took my books.

Then she took my breath.

I can't shake the feeling that I've known her before.

Maybe in another life.

But I don't have time for love while I'm trying to make partner.

Jax Wilder

Step into Coral Cove, where the sun meets the moon in a spellbinding sapphic romance that will set your heart ablaze with forbidden love.

Every lunar eclipse in Coral Cove offers a fleeting moment of magic where Ophelia's memories are restored, allowing her to remember her for Lilly and the life they once shared. Can the Sun and Moon find a way to be together despite the gods' decree?

Additional Books by Rainbow Quartz Publishing

Additional Titles by Jax Wilder

Coral Cove Series
Sleighed by Love
Harvesting Love
Dawning Desire
Knead You Now
Haunted by Her
Perfect Lover Spell

Tarot Fantasies Series
The Devil's Temptations
Strength of the Beast
Hanged Passions
Death's Embrace

Miranda Levi
From A Youth A Fountain Did Flow
The Sea Withdrew
A Tear In Time
Mo(ther) Na(ture)
In Orion's Hands

Jackson Anhalt
From The 911 Files

Jax Wilder

Lorelai Hamilton

Find Your Bliss
Teenage Witch's Grimoire
Tarot Reflection Journal
Tarot Refection Journal Coloring The Tarot
The Eclectic Witch's Grimoire
Dream Journal
Teenage Tarot
Tarot Tales and Magic Spells
Arcane In Verse

Isla Watts

A Fairy Bad Day
Surprise! You're a Vampire
Gorgeous, Gorgeous, Gorgons
Mork The Handsome Orc
Adopted By Werewolves
Bite Me If You Can
That's The Spirit!

Rose Dawson's Book Journals

My Time With The Fairies
Enchanted Escapades
Enchanted Escapades
Dewey Decimal Diaries
Siren's Songbook
Pride and Prejudice
Bibliophile's Bounty

Harvesting Love

Book of Books Journal
Pages & Passages Reading Journal
Bookworm's Companion Reading Journal & Tracker

Acknowledgments

I wanted to write a story that doesn't often get told. Gay romance, gay experiences, and gay emotions are just as valid as anyone else's. I needed Park's story to be happy and uplifting, with a supportive and fun family. This is a world that can exist if we all just work to be a little bit more tolerant of each other.

Thank you MT, who helped me realize that this story needed to be told. What started as a conversation at a queer market turned into a full saucy story.

And a special thank you to my sister. I love you.

Thank you to my readers. You are the reason I do this.

About the Author

Jax Wilder is a passionate romance author hailing from a charming small town nestled in the picturesque Pacific Northwest. With a heart full of love and an unyielding belief in the power of happily ever afters, Jax weaves enchanting tales of love and connection that leave readers captivated.

Jax's novels are a reflection of the commitment shared to celebrating the magic of all love.

Afterall, Love is Love.